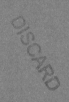

THE SECRET OF THE GREAT HOUDINI

For Graham Burnett Burleigh
(May he find his own "secret" in the years to come!)
—R. B.

To Uri, my first teacher
—L. G.

Atheneum Books for Young Readers
An imprint of Simon & Schuster
Children's Publishing Division
1230 Avenue of the Americas
New York, New York 10020
Text copyright © 2002 by Robert Burleigh
Illustrations copyright © 2002 by Leonid Gore
Book design by Ann Bobco
The text of this book is set in Centaur MT.
The illustrations in this book are set in pastels and ink.
Printed in Hong Kong
1 2 3 4 5 6 7 8 9 10
Library of Congress Cataloging-in-Publication Data
Burleigh, Robert.
The secret of the Great Houdini / by Robert Burleigh ; illustrated by
Leonid Gore.—1st ed.
p.   cm.
Summary: As Sam and Uncle Ezra watch, the Great Houdini escapes from a trunk
at the bottom of the river. Includes factual information about Houdini
and his career as a magician and escape artist.
ISBN 0-689-83267-2
1. Houdini, Harry, 1874-1926—Juvenile fiction. [1. Houdini, Harry, 1874–1926—
Fiction. 2. Escape artists—Fiction. 3. Magicians—Fiction. 3. Magicians—Fiction.]
I. Gore, Leonid, ill. II. Title.
PZ7.B9244 Se 2002
[Fic]—dc21   00-038057

FIRST EDITION

ROBERT BURLEIGH

THE SECRET OF THE GREAT HOUDINI

LEONID GORE

ATHENEUM BOOKS FOR YOUNG READERS

NEW YORK LONDON TORONTO SYDNEY SINGAPORE

Sam leans forward and gazes down
at the cold water sloshing against the pier,
so cold and deep it makes his skin feel bumpy.

"Is he afraid?

 Going—in there—in a locked trunk?"

"Everyone's afraid sometimes," Uncle Ezra answers.

"The Great Houdini goes where he has to go."

Behind his uncle, Sam sees people arriving.

Then suddenly, every head turns.

The crowd opens a narrow pathway.

A bubble of voices rises up and pops into words:

"He's coming!" "There he is!" "Look, look!

Houdini! Houdini! The Great Houdini!"

I am Houdini.

I have the power.

I am one whom nothing
can contain.

Do you believe me?

Houdini walks out to the end of the pier.

He walks on the balls of his feet, lightly.

As if he is part human and part cat.

He turns and raises his arms, and the crowd cheers.

He removes his robe and stands in the sun.

He wears a bathing suit. His hands are empty.

He brings nothing with him. Houdini. Alone.

I am Houdini.

I escape the hold of all things.

I free myself.

Do you believe me?

He nods, and two men approach with
long chains.
Together they wrap the chains around
Houdini's body.
Two more men fasten his wrists with
handcuffs.
And now the men lift Houdini and place
him inside a large metal trunk.

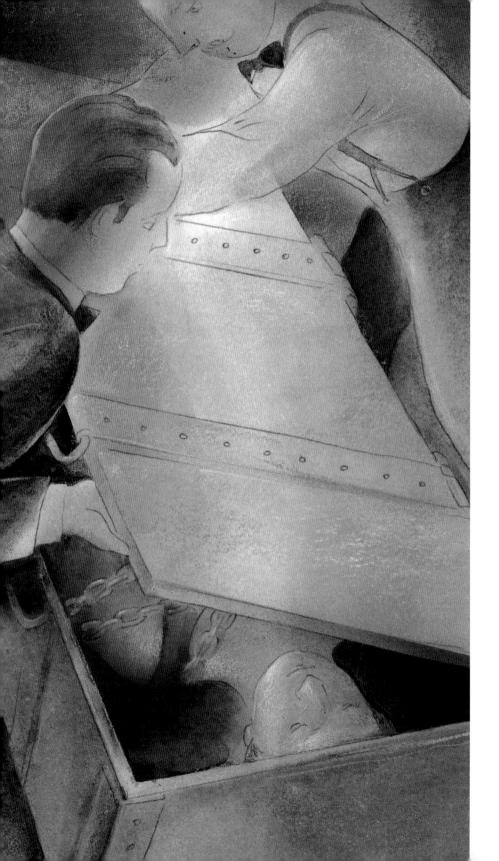

The crowd is so still that even from far off
the lock's tiny click can be heard as it snaps shut.

The arm of a small crane comes down
and hoists the trunk into the air
and out over the water.
Everything stops.

Sam reaches for his uncle Ezra's hand.
"He's waiting," his uncle whispers.
 Uncle Ezra's eyes are fixed on the trunk, too.
"The Great Houdini does nothing—until he
 hears 'the voice.'"

I, Houdini.

I know the secret.

I hear a small voice.

Do you believe me?

Sam looks up at his uncle.
"What's the voice?" Sam whispers back.
"It comes from in here." His uncle
  points to Sam's chest.
"It says: 'I have worked hard.'
  It says: 'I have prepared myself and believe
  in myself.'
  It says: 'I'm ready.'"

A muffled thump comes from the trunk,
  as if feet were kicking at its inner walls.
"He's ready," Uncle Ezra says. "That's the signal."

Slowly the trunk is lowered, and the crowd
lets out a gasp.
For a brief moment, it rocks back and
forth on the water.
Then, with one last rusty corner pointing
to the sky, it dips and disappears.

"It's cold. So cold and dark."
Sam's thoughts come out in shivery words.
Somewhere out of sight the trunk with
its human cargo is tumbling noiselessly
into the black!

"Ah." Uncle Ezra raises his bushy eyebrows.
"Darkness and cold are in the bones of
the Great Houdini."
As Sam watches the last ripples ride
toward the pier's edge,

his uncle tells him how the boy Houdini rode freight trains
across America,
seeking work, huddled against the icy walls of boxcars;
how he slept winter nights in hobo camps;
how he joined the circus;
how he trained by himself for hours and hours;
how he learned to hang upside down;
how he learned to pick up small objects with just his teeth—

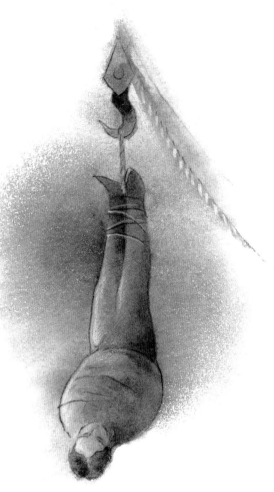

"It's a trick, Uncle Ez, isn't it?"

"A trick?"
Uncle Ezra smiles and straightens the brim of his bowler hat.
"No.
Houdini calls it—his *secret.*
He never calls it a trick."

Cry fake. Doubt.

Deny what you see with your very eyes.

Still, I slip through the clutch of iron.

My quick fingers know the meanings of things!

Do you believe me?

A man behind them with a megaphone bellows:

"THIRTY SECONDS AT THE BOTTOM OF THE RIVER. BOUND IN CHAINS. THE GREAT HOUDINI."

"The chains, Uncle Ez. They're too heavy.
He'll never—"
"Chains are silk shirts to the Great
Houdini." Uncle Ez chuckles.
"He puts them on—and he takes them off."

And as Sam tries to imagine the trunk,
sinking into a huge mouth of river muck,
his uncle tells how the Great Houdini,
strapped in a straitjacket, once hung from
a skyscraper;
how he dangled by his ankles;
how thousands craned their necks as he
spun there,
blown back and forth by the wind,
and wriggled until he unwound himself—

"ONE MINUTE AT THE BOTTOM OF THE RIVER. HANDCUFFED. THE GREAT HOUDINI."

Voices in the crowd begin murmuring:

"He won't make it out."

"He's a goner."

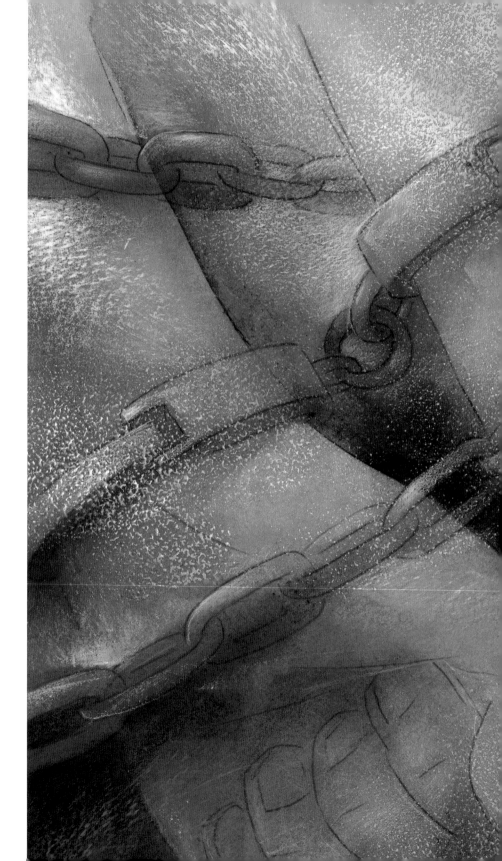

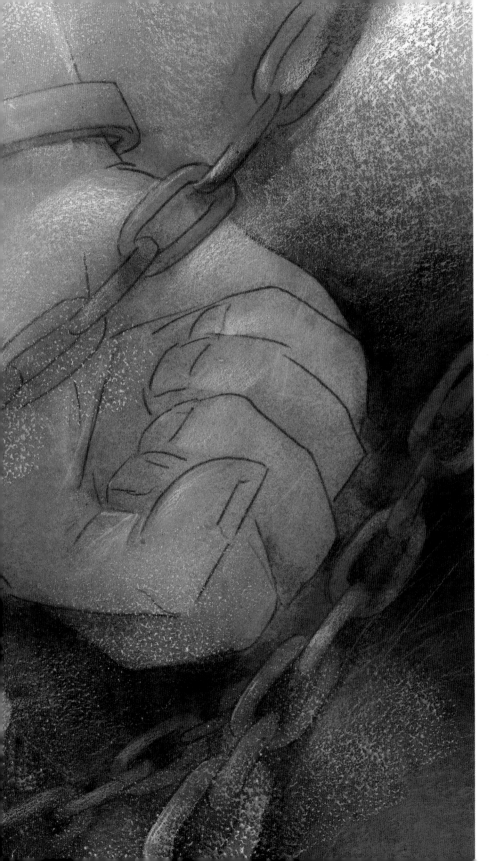

Sam looks at his own thin wrists.
"Handcuffs?"
Uncle Ezra looks out of the corner of his eye.
"Handcuffs are paper bracelets to
the Great Houdini."
And his uncle tells how a jailer once
challenged Houdini,
locked him, handcuffed, inside a cell
and walked off, smiling and sure as sugar;
and how the Great Houdini not only freed himself—
but eight other prisoners, too,
just for the show of it—

"ONE MINUTE AND THIRTY SECONDS AT THE BOTTOM OF THE RIVER. LOCKED IN A TRUNK. THE GREAT HOUDINI."

Locked in a trunk. Oh, locked in a trunk!
Sam remembers the little click.
He remembers the sad, hollow, good-bye knock of Houdini's foot signal.
He can feel the rough metal of the inner walls.
He feels feet kicking, kicking, kicking wildly in the darkness.
He feels Houdini's body twisting sideways.
He feels terrified fingers trying
to pick and claw and force the lock.

"He's bolted in," he says weakly to his uncle.
But Uncle Ezra just tweaks the end of his mustache.
"A locked box is simply a house to the Great Houdini:
He finds the door—"

Mysterious is the water I move through,

(deeper than all of my doubters)

as a fish swims in the sea.

Do you believe?

"Just as he found his way out
of a government mail pouch in San Francisco,
an iron boiler in Toledo,
a triple-locked safe in Trenton,
a zinc-lined piano box in Buffalo,
a water-filled milk can in Philadelphia,
and—oh—from a coffin in Boston
whose lid the audience members
themselves had nailed down—"

AT THE BOTTOM

RIVER. TWO.

TWO MINUTES.

HOUDINI."

Sam isn't listening anymore.

He holds his own breath and counts.

He is down there himself now: Sam,

inside the airlessness with horrible thrashing,

the cold, inky water seeping through the cracks,

and a vise crushing his lungs, squeezing the seconds out:

Twenty-four, twenty-five, twenty-six, twenty-seven——

Somewhere, panicked voices are shouting:

"Call for an ambulance!"

"Someone dive in and help!"

"Please, please!"

I am Houdini.

I confound the sleeper.

I amaze the unwilling-to-believe.

I mystify the all-too-sure.

Sam looks straight ahead, into the water.

"He'll die," is all he says.

Thirty-one, thirty-two, thirty-three, thirty——

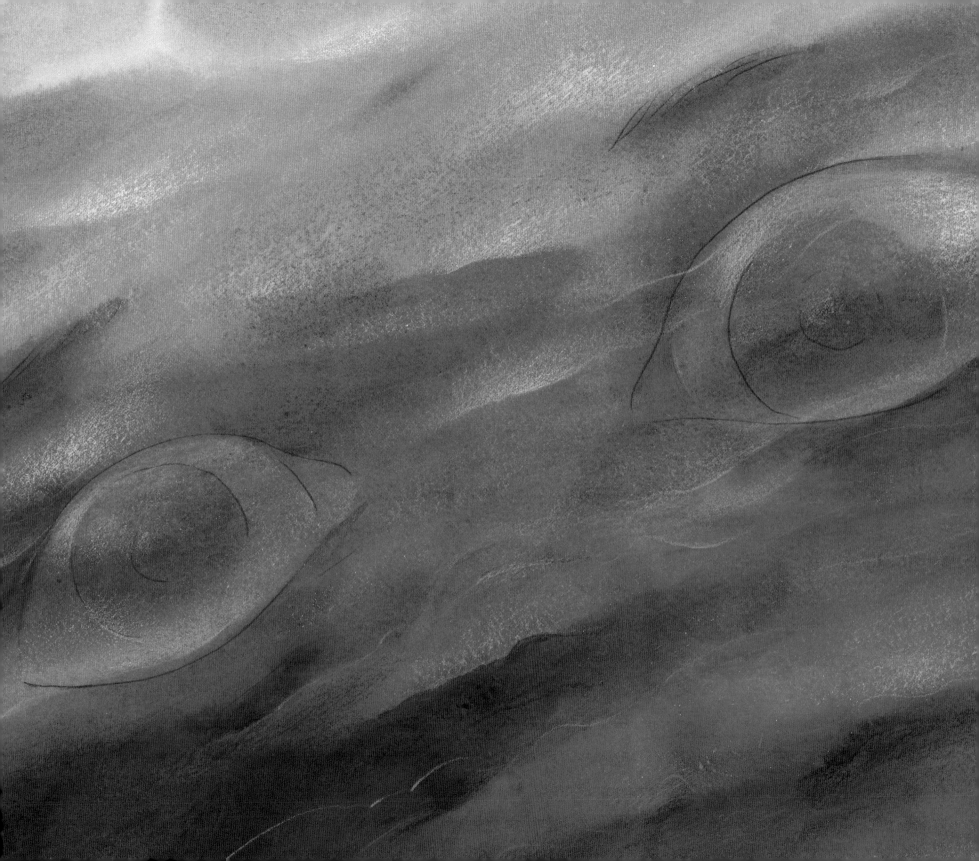

Just then the dark river spreads
as if a small tunnel had opened.
Spray, a flash on the surface,
white foam—
and Houdini's pale face, gasping,
pokes like a dolphin into a sky of
thunderous applause.
Sam sucks in air, too, clapping and
screaming with all the rest.

But, see, the river opens.

I rise into the light.

I blink.

I shake my chains at you

who are invisibly chained!

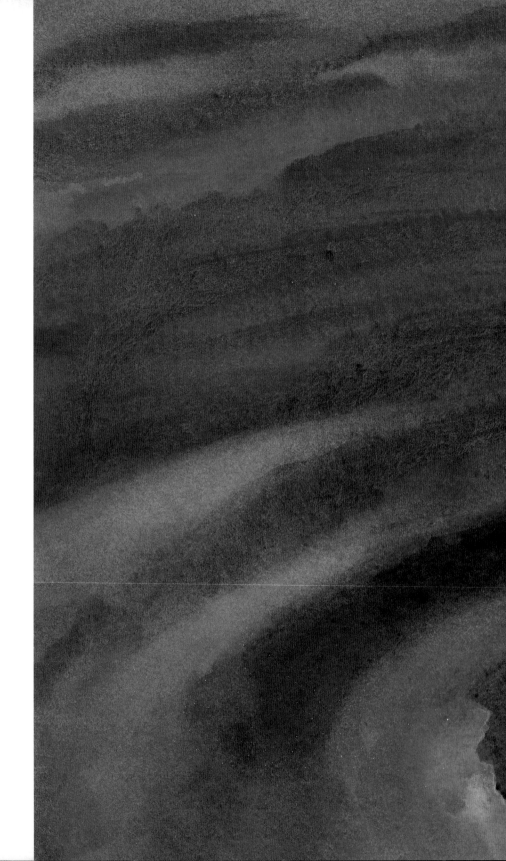

A motorboat putters into view.
Houdini, clutching the chains
and the handcuffs,
awkwardly climbs the rope ladder.
Someone throws a large towel over his
shoulders.
He faces the shore. He takes a deep bow.
Then, he raises the chains and handcuffs
high over his head.
Defiantly he flings them out over the water.

Uncle Ezra smiles.
"Aha!
He's won again, eh?"

"His secret, Uncle Ez."
Sam looks up.
"Tell me his secret."

"I don't think it's one thing," the older man replies.
"It's a mix of many things.
It's bravery and hard work and practice
and wanting to be or do something so very much that—"

Uncle Ezra pauses and gazes straight into Sam's eyes.
"But maybe you shouldn't wonder so much about *his* secret," he says.
"What's really important is finding *your* secret—
something that becomes like a seed inside you—
that will grow as you grow up."

Sam looks back at his uncle and nods.
All at once there is a strange, light, jumping-up feeling in his feet.
The boat carrying Houdini moves down the river
as Sam squints into the setting sun.

I am Houdini.

I am one whom nothing can contain.

I free myself.

Do you believe me now?

At last?

Houdini stands waving at the edge of the boat.
Is he waving to him?
To Sam?
Sam holds on to his uncle's hand and, leaping into the air,
with his other arm, waves back.

AFTERWORD

Harry Houdini was born Erich Weiss in Budapest, Hungary, in 1874. His parents, however, soon came to the United States, where young Erich grew up in Appleton, Wisconsin. Even as a boy, he showed great skill and interest in magic. After working in various circuses and vaudeville shows, he began his career as a magician. He took his name from the name of a famous French magician, Jean-Eugène Robert-Houdin. Although skilled in many areas of magic, Houdini became especially famous for his escapes. He escaped from handcuffs, jail cells, safes, locked trunks, and straitjackets. How did he do it? Did he have—as many believed—superhuman powers? We do know that he had an expert knowledge of all locks. He was also strong, bold, and fearless. But Houdini never told his secret, and so in some cases his escape methods remain unknown even into the present time. He died in 1926, after allowing himself to be punched in the stomach (in order to prove his bodily strength) by a young student and suffering from a ruptured appendix. But even now—many years after his death—the name Houdini still suggests the mysterious power to break free!

DATE			